The Scared Little Angel

The Scared Little Angel

Cyan Brown

Illustrated by Floris Eloff

Reach
PUBLISHERS

Published by Cyan Brown using Reach Publishers' services,
P O Box 1384, Wandsbeck, South Africa, 3631

Edited by Rendale Snow for Reach Publishers
Cover designed by Reach Publishers
Website: www.reachpublishers.org
E-mail: reach@reachpublish.co.za

Reach
PUBLISHERS

Cyan Brown

authorcyanbrown@gmail.com

Illustrations by Floris Eloff

This book is dedicated to my grandmother,
Gloria (Darling) Brown.

There once was a little angel as sweet as pie
who lived up amongst the fluffy clouds so high.

She was different from others though, that's no lie;
she walked everywhere while other angels flew by.
Because this little angel couldn't flutter at all,
her mouth turned down, her insides were heartsore.

The other angels looked at her and wanted to cry.
"You cannot touch the sky little angel,"
they would say with a sigh and sad eyes.

The little angel was loved but left out by law
because flying was the greatest gift of all.

She dragged her rose-gold wings behind her in shame
because she was actually the only one to blame.

She had stood on the edge trembling with fright
but too scared to take a step forward to attempt flight.

What if she fell and tumbled forever
or even worse, fell right out of Heaven.

Too scared to leap to reach for more,
the little angel stayed grounded, pitied by all.

One day out walking in the Earthly field
amongst rainbow flowers, where bees
swooped and reeled,
she came across a fish that had flopped
out of the water.

Running over, she scooped him up and
put him back like they had taught her.
Fish couldn't be happy outside of the river.

She knew he could have dried out and let out a shiver.
"What were you doing silly little fish!"
as he returned with not a splash but a splish.

"I'm tired of being beneath," was his sad reply.
"I wanted to leap to swish my tail high."

Kneeling in wonder, she examined the fish.
She realised we all wanted and wished.
"You risk your life for what? To jump tall?"
"I'd rather know freedom than nothing at all!"

With those last words he swam away.
The little angel was silent; she had nothing to say.

For the first time she saw her fear for what it was.
She was the servant and it was her boss.

The ground became a cage and her
wings a constant taunt
of what she could have if fear didn't haunt.

On the seventh day of pacing and
thinking these thoughts
she made a decision, a desperate resignation of sorts.

She came to a ridge of the highest mountain of all.
Looking down into the unknown, her
stomach felt the fall.
Her insides were trembling, her tummy a ball.

Her fear lived inside her now, waging a war.
But she knew in her heart if she didn't at least try,
she would forever be wishing and watching others fly.

Safe though she was, her life steady and calming,
she knew deep inside, doing nothing was harming.
She shook out her wings and straightened her spine.

It was time she decided for things to be
better than fine.
With a leap she took a chance, reaching out for more.

She took the fish's advice and she finally jumped tall.
And yes, she did fall and questioned herself.

Have I sacrificed everything to only lose myself?

But suddenly her wings snapped out on either side.
She swooped in the air, carried on the wind like a tide.

"I did it!" she cried,
wings spread wide.

So the risk may be great and failure daunting
but she'd be lesser without and the unknown haunting.

By fighting her fear, she had found her calling.
She shouted, "Flying is so much better than walking!"

So the angels rejoiced, taking to the sky
to be with the little angel that could finally fly.

There is nothing wrong with a life back on the ground
but don't miss out because fear will always be around.

Reach out for more,

Be brave,
Jump tall.

Printed in Great Britain
by Amazon